WHISPERS OF THE UNHEARD

WHISPERS OF THE UNHEARD: FINDING STRENGTH IN SILENT BATTLES

DISHA BHATIA

For everyone fighting battles no one else sees,

For those who find strength in their silence and
resilience in their struggles—

May you know that even in the quietest moments, you
are never truly alone.

*This is for you—keepers of hope, seekers of
light, and silent warriors.*

Contents

Contents

Foreword

In a world where stories are often told loudly and boldly, there are countless voices that remain unheard. The quiet ones. The ones who fight their battles in silence, who carry the weight of their struggles without anyone noticing. Whispers of the Unheard is for them.

This book is an exploration of the invisible, the unnoticed—of those who endure pain, hardship, and grief, but whose struggles are hidden beneath a surface of quiet strength. It is a story that seeks to give a voice to the voiceless, a face to the faceless, and hope to those who feel they've been overlooked.

The protagonist, Meera, embodies this silent resilience. Her journey mirrors that of countless individuals who live with invisible struggles. While others may not see her pain, she navigates through life with a quiet determination. This book captures the rawness of those internal battles and the courage it takes to keep moving forward, even when the world doesn't seem to notice.

This novel is a tribute to the silent warriors—the ones who don't have the words or the voice to speak their pain but who, nonetheless, find ways to keep going. It's for anyone who has ever felt alone, as though their story is not worth telling or their struggles too small to matter.

Through Meera's journey, I hope to remind readers that their pain is valid and their strength undeniable. Even when it feels like no one is listening, there are whispers of hope that reach us when we least expect it. You are not invisible, and your story is worth sharing.

May this book serve as a reminder that, even in the quietest moments, we are never truly alone. You are seen, you are heard, and your journey matters.

Thank you for joining Meera on this journey. May her story inspire you to keep going, even in silence.

Prologue

In a world where words are often loud and voices are too quick to be heard, there exists a silence—one that carries the weight of countless untold stories. It is the silence of those who struggle quietly, who endure pain that remains unseen by others. These are the whispers of the unheard: the voices that never reach the surface, hidden beneath layers of resilience, fear, and self-doubt.

"Whispers of the Unheard" is a journey into that silence. It is a journey that begins with the realization that sometimes, the loudest battles are fought in the quietest corners of the soul. It is a reminder that strength does not always need to be visible, and healing often starts in the most unexpected ways.

This story is not just for those who have been through pain, but for everyone who has ever felt the sting of being unnoticed. It's for the ones who keep fighting when no one is watching, who carry their burdens in silence because they have no other choice. But this is not just a story about suffering—it is one of hope, resilience, and finding light in the darkest of places.

In these pages, you will meet Meera, a girl whose silence speaks louder than her words. As she grapples with her own hidden struggles, she discovers a way to connect with others who, too, fight in silence. Through anonymous notes and quiet gestures, she learns that even in the moments when it feels like no one is listening, there is always someone else who understands. And together, they create a network of strength, forged in the unspoken.

This is not just Meera's story—it is the story of us all. The story of the strength we find when we allow ourselves to be heard, even if it is just through whispers. And perhaps, through these whispers, we will come to realize that we are never as alone as we feel.

● x ●

I

The Weight Of Perfection

Meera sat by the window, staring out at the world beyond the glass. The evening sky was painted in hues of pink and orange, a fleeting masterpiece that would soon give way to the darkness of night. To an outsider, it was a beautiful sight—serene, peaceful. But to Meera, it was just another day, another sunset, another reminder that she was trapped in a life that wasn't her own.

Inside the house buzzed with the sounds of routine life in a middle-class family. Her mother was in the kitchen, cooking dinner. The scent of spices wafted through the air, comforting yet oppressive. The voice of a news anchor echoed in the living room as her father watched the current affairs on TV while sipping his cup of chai—it was a routine that Meera had grown to despise.

She turned away from the window and caught a reflection in the glass. The eyes that made contact with hers felt familiar yet somehow unfamiliar. The smile that she forced every day, the bright eyes that looked into her pitch-black ones, fluttering, flickering, and flinching—the eyes that always masked her darkness—were concealed behind the meticulously braided hair that her mother believed was a mark of discipline and proper upbringing. It was all a charade. A disguise Meera had perfected over the years, a mask that concealed the real Meera from everyone.

On the surface, Meera was the perfect daughter—the daughter every parent would wish for. Obedient, studious, creative, and respectful—these were synonyms for Meera. Her grades were always at the top of the class, her teachers always spoke highly of her, and her relatives often praised her for being a "good girl." But none of them knew the truth. The truth that she was hiding from everyone: the heavy weight of their expectations, the weight of being the perfect daughter, the good girl, and the top student. How suffocating the pressure to be perfect had become.

Meera had always been an achiever. From a young age, she had excelled in everything she did, whether it was academics, sports, or extracurricular activities. Her parents had always been proud of her, and she had worked hard to keep it that way. But somewhere in her mind, she knew that the joy of learning and the thrill of discovery were being replaced by a relentless drive to meet the ever-growing expectations of her parents and society.

As she sat at her desk, opened her notebook, and stared at the blank pages of literature—her favorite subject, the one that had once brought her so much joy—she now felt it was a burden to complete. The words seemed to have lost their magic. She was tired, tired of fighting with herself, tired of fulfilling the expectations of those around her, tired of maintaining the image of the "perfect" daughter. Her passion for literature, which had once felt like a lifeline, now seemed overshadowed by the weight of expectations that stifled her creativity and joy.

She glanced at the clock. Nearly 7 PM—the time to start getting herself ready for the next day's lessons. But all she craved was to escape, escape from the reality that was dragging her down. To immerse herself in poetry, to let the words and verses carry her away from the brutal world she was tired of. The only thing that brought her peace was poetry—the only time she could truly be herself and express her emotions freely. But even that was a secret—a passion she kept hidden from her parents, who saw it as a waste of time. The solace she yearned for was the thought of scribbling verses, which was the only way to get away from the relentless academic pressure that defined her life.

Meera sighed and picked up her pencil. She started focusing and blinked away the tears that threatened to spill over. She wouldn't cry. She had to be strong. She had to be perfect.

But deep down, she knew she couldn't wear this mask forever. The mask she wore was cracking, the weight of the expectations getting heavier with each passing day. And as the sun dipped below the horizon, casting the room in shadow, Meera couldn't shake the feeling that something inside her was about to break.

II

The Weight of
Silence

The morning sun streamed through the curtains, casting a warm glow over Meera's room. The soft chirping of birds outside should have brought her comfort, but instead, it only heightened the sense of dread that had settled in her chest. She had barely slept the night before, tossing and turning as her mind raced with thoughts she couldn't control. Every time she closed her eyes, she saw the faces of her parents, her teachers, her friends—all expecting something from her, all waiting for her to be the girl they believed she was.

The alarm clock buzzed sharply, pulling her out of her thoughts. Meera sighed and got out of bed, mechanically going through the motions of her daily routine. She brushed her teeth, washed her face, and tied her hair into a neat braid. As she stood in front of the mirror and saw the same tired eyes staring back at her, she noticed dark circles under them now, a testament to another sleepless night she had suffered, afraid of the stares. She quickly looked away.

At the breakfast table, there sat her parents, engrossed in their daily routine. Her father was making comments about the political scandal from the information printed in the newspaper, while her mother flipped the pages of magazines while having chai. She noticed Meera's presence and said, "Meera, finish your breakfast quickly, or you'll be late for school," without looking up at her. Meera replied, "Yes, Maa," picking up her spoon and eating the food, which tasted like ash in her mouth. She forced herself to eat, as leaving unfinished food on her plate would lead to questions—questions she didn't have the energy to answer.

"Don't forget about your math tutoring after school," her father added, unaware of the mental turmoil inside her mind.

Meera nodded, despite the fact that the thought of spending more hours on numbers and equations made her stomach turn. She hated math, but she couldn't tell them. She couldn't tell them how much the thought of numbers and equations drained her because all they cared about were the grades—and her future—the future they had already planned for her.

As she walked into the school, trying to push her thoughts away and distracting herself by following the rhythm of her footsteps, the weight on her chest was always there, a reminder that she wasn't living her own life.

The school day passed in a blur. Meera went from class to class, taking notes, answering questions, doing everything expected of her. But her mind was elsewhere, lost in the pages of the notebook where she scribbled her thoughts, her pain from the night before.

During lunch, she sat with her friends, pretending to listen to their conversations about their plans for the evening, the weekends, and the gossip. She gave them a smile and nodded in all the right places, though her heart wasn't in it. She felt disconnected.

"Meera, are you okay?" her best friend Tamanna asked, noticing the unusual silence from the one who was usually a chatterbox.

"I'm fine," Meera answered, forcing a smile.

A lie she said every time. As the day went on, the weight in her chest grew heavier, suffocating her. As the last bell rang, signaling the end of the day, Meera could hardly breathe.

The tutoring session was just as torturous as she had imagined. The numbers danced in front of her, mocking her, reminding her how much she hated them. The tutor rattled on and on, but Meera could hardly focus. All she wanted was to escape, to run away from these expectations and responsibilities.

When she finally got home, wearing the mask as always, it was already dark outside. Her parents were in the living room, watching TV. They didn't ask her how her day was, didn't notice the exhaustion etched into her features, didn't notice what was actually behind the mask she wore every day so that no one would ask her questions—questions she was even tired of finding the answers to. They were too wrapped up in their own world, too focused on their own lives, not knowing how their daughter was suffering.

Meera just went straight to her room, closing the door behind her. She didn't even bother turning on the light because for her, darkness was a comfort.

There the girl sat, shattered, surrounded by fear and gloom.
Her silence spoke something,
her eyes teary and tired now,

weeks ago, they were full of joy.
But life had shifted somehow,
dreams turned into mere ploys.
Her laughter, once a melody sweet,
now echoed in the past,
her heart, once steady in its beat,
now breaks, each moment, vast.

The words came out easily, as they always did when she let herself go. But as she wrote, she felt a pang of sadness, knowing that no one would ever read these lines. No one would ever know the silent battle she fought every day. No one would ever be able to understand the expectations and responsibilities that were killing her.

When she finally put the pen down, the room was completely dark—darkness that held the loneliness and the emptiness. Meera stared at the page, her heart heavy with the weight of her own words. She knew she couldn't keep going like this, that something had to change. But what? And how?

The answers she was tired of finding. She didn't have the answers. All she had with her were the loneliness, the feeling of emptiness, the pain, and the verses on the pages that she couldn't speak out loud. And as she lay down to sleep, which was long overdue, she couldn't shake the feeling that the darkness was closing in, inch by inch, until there was no light left at all.

III
The Weight of Expectations

The school buzzed with the usual energy of the students, rushing to their classrooms, some laughing and sharing bits of gossip with their friends. Meera moved through the crowd like a ghost, her presence unnoticed, just like her mental turmoil, her mind elsewhere, thinking about the verses she had penned down the night before. Each day felt more like a burden, a series of tasks to be completed rather than moments to be lived. The joy of living had been replaced by just existing. The joy she once felt in learning, in discovering new things, had been replaced by a relentless, grinding monotony.

In her science class, Meera sat at the back, her notebook open but untouched. The teacher droned on about the chemical reactions, the formulas scrawled across the board in neat, precise handwriting. But to Meera, they were just symbols, meaningless. She knew she should be paying attention, taking notes, and preparing for her upcoming exams that everyone kept reminding her about. But her mind drifted, slipping into the verses she had composed.

"I am the shadow in the light,

Hiding in plain sight,

A whisper lost in the wind,

A truth I can't rescind..."

She wrote them in the margins of her notebook, tiny scribbles that no one would notice. It was a small act, her way of clinging to the part of herself that she felt alive. But even that small comfort was fleeting, overshadowed by the looming presence of her teacher at the front of the room.

"Meera," the teacher called out, breaking her chains of thought. "Can you explain the process of oxidation?"

Startled, Meera blinked and looked up. Seeing everyone staring at her, waiting for her to answer, made her heart race, and panic rose in her chest. She knew the answer, of course, as she had studied about it a dozen times, but the words were not coming out. She didn't know how to form the words to answer. Her mind was blank, a vast emptiness where there should have been knowledge.

"Oxidation is... um... it's when..." she stammered, her voice trailing off.

The teacher frowned, a look of disappointment clearly visible on her face, as the expectations were not fulfilled this time. "You need to focus, Meera. This is important material."

Meera nodded, her cheeks burning with shame. She lowered her head, hiding behind her long, dark hair, and tried to shrink into her seat. The rest of the lesson passed in a haze, the teacher's voice a distant hum as Meera battled the overwhelming sense of failure that had taken hold of her.

As the bell rang, signaling the end of the class, Meera quickly left the room, eager to ignore the stares of judgment from her peers. She found a quiet spot in the school courtyard, away from the bustling crowd. She sat on the ground, trembling in fear. The words of the teacher haunted her, a reminder of how far she had fallen from the image everyone had of her as the "PERFECT" student.

For the first time, she felt the pressure of holding everything together becoming too much to bear. The weight of expectations, the constant need to be perfect, was suffocating her, making it hard for her to breathe. And now, even the one thing that she had always relied on—her academic prowess—was slipping away from her. She felt the cracks in her carefully constructed facade widening.

As she sat there, staring at the ground, Meera wondered how much longer she could keep this up. How much longer she could pretend that everything was fine when inside, she was breaking apart. The thought of leaving everything behind and the weight of expectations was terrifying, but it brought a strange sense of relief. What if she let everything she had built with years of hard work, the responsibilities, the expectations, crumble? She wouldn't have to pretend anymore. Maybe then, she could finally be herself and feel the freedom of living her own life, at least for once.

But that was a dangerous thought, one she couldn't afford to entertain. Not yet. Not when so much was at stake. So, with a heavy heart, Meera pushed the doubt aside, buried it deep within her, and prepared to face another day of living someone else's life, another day of trying to fulfill the expectations, and another day of pretending that everything was fine.

IV
Hidden Struggles Within

Meera's walk home from school was as familiar as tracing the lines of her own palm, something she could almost do with her eyes closed. The streets were crowded as usual—buses honking, children running around. But it all felt distant to her, like she was watching it happen from far away. The noise and movements didn't touch her; they couldn't break through the walls she had built around herself.

As she walked, thinking about today's science class, the looks of disappointment were messing with her mind. The words of her science teacher were making her feel vulnerable, and her failure to answer the question was haunting her. She was supposed to know the answer, as she always did. But that day, her mind had gone blank, like all the knowledge she had crammed had slipped away.

The truth was, it wasn't just that one moment in class. Lately, she had been feeling more and more distant from everyone and everything. Her studies, her parents, her friends—it all felt like a blur, like she was just existing instead of living, one of her worst fears becoming true. She knew she couldn't share her mental turmoil with anyone. She couldn't show her weak side, at least not when everyone expected her to be perfect.

At home, Meera slipped into her usual routine. She greeted her parents and forced a smile, the same smile she always wore, one that hid all her pain and weakness. As the aroma of spices hit her nose, her steps led her to the kitchen to talk with her mother, while her father sat at the dining table, reading the newspaper. A typical evening in their household, where the weight of unspoken expectations hung in the air.

"Did you finish all your assignments?" her mother asked, without looking up from her cooking as soon as Meera entered the kitchen.

"Yes, maa," she answered automatically, even though she hadn't touched her homework since school ended. The thought of sitting down with her books again made her feel exhausted. She knew she would have to do it eventually, though there was no escape from the cycle of endless studying and exams. As her future depended on it, according to her father, who glanced up from the paper and asked, "How's school? Any tests coming up?"

Meera nodded, feeling her stomach tighten. "Yes, we have a science test next week."

"Good," her father said, his voice calm yet firm. "Make sure you're well-prepared. We can't afford any distractions, Meera. Your future depends on these exams."

That word—future—felt like a boulder pressing down on her. Everyone talked about her future as if it were the only thing that mattered, as if everything she did now was just to reach a faraway goal she hadn't even picked for herself. But what about now? What about how she felt in this moment?

After dinner, Meera retreated to her room. Closing the door behind her, she sank onto her bed, staring at the textbooks, which felt like they were mocking her, reminding her of the expectations she had to meet, driving her insane.

But instead of picking up her books, she reached for the notebook under her pillow, the one in which she wrote what her heart was feeling without fear of someone ever knowing. The one in which she wrote her poetry. The only thing that made her feel free. Her poetry was full of the thoughts she couldn't say aloud, the emotions she kept hidden from everyone.

"There I see her once again,
Whimpering in pain, squealing in the dark,
Hiding her scars, drinking and smoking out her past.
Broken inside,
Still smiling, but I know inside
She is fighting,
Living but not alive,
Drowning in a world of fear and loathing,
Broken soul,
Struggling to be fine."

The words flowed from her pencil effortlessly, like they had been waiting for this moment to escape. As she wrote, Meera felt a brief sense of relief, a small spark of hope that maybe, just maybe, she could survive the overwhelming pressure. But even as she filled the page with her thoughts, a nagging voice in the back of her mind reminded her that writing wouldn't save her from the future that was closing in on her, faster and faster.

The weight of silence, the burden of unspoken fears, was growing heavier with each passing day.

V

The Strain of Perfection

Meera sat at her desk, ignoring the turmoil happening inside her. Her mind was tired, but she couldn't afford to stop, as every test, every project, every grade was a measure of her worth in the eyes of her parents, teachers, and society.

Her phone buzzed with notifications from her classmates discussing the upcoming exam. Meera's chest tightened. She had always been the one others looked up to – "The Model Student." People assumed that everything was easy for her, that she never struggled. But what they didn't see was the endless hours she spent fighting against her anxiety, the fear of failure that kept her awake at night.

A knock interrupted her train of thought. Her mother peeked in, a proud smile on her face. "Meera, are you studying for the exam tomorrow? You will do great, as always."

"Yes, Maa, I'm just going over everything one last time," Meera answered, forcing a smile.

The door closed softly, and the smile vanished from her face. She wanted to scream, to let out all the frustration she had kept inside for so long—the fear of failure that was building inside her—but she couldn't. She had to maintain the image of the perfect daughter, the one who never complained about anything. To everyone else, she was unbreakable. Inside, though, she was starting to crack in the way that the joy of learning had once been a source of curiosity and excitement, but now felt like a competition, a race she couldn't afford to lose. The pressure of perfection had killed it all. Every time she opened a book, it was no longer about discovering something new—it was about getting better, faster, and smarter than everyone else. The love for school was being replaced with the suffocation of the weight of expectations.

Meera glanced at the mirror on her desk. The façade of neatly braided hair, the spotless uniform, the perfect posture. Behind it, she felt like she was falling apart. The girl staring back at her looked tired, hollow. Her eyes reflected the feeling of emptiness and helplessness, which no one, other than her, could see.

Taking a deep breath, Meera closed her textbook and leaned back in her chair. For just a moment, she allowed herself to pause, to let the silence settle around her. But even in that silence, the voices of expectation still echoed in her mind.

"You can't stop now. You have to be the best. You have to be perfect."

And so, with trembling hands and a heavy heart, Meera reopened her book and began to study again, knowing that the strain of perfection was slowly crushing her, breaking her, but still unable to let go.

VI

A Moment of Imperfection

The next morning, Meera walked through the school gates, her bag slung over her shoulder, the weight of her textbooks a constant reminder of the responsibilities she bore, but it was nothing compared to the weight of expectations. As the morning sunlight filtered through the trees lining the pathway, it felt like a bright façade covering the storm brewing inside her. The chatter of her classmates filled the air, laughter mingling with the sound of the school bell ringing, but she felt detached. She felt like an observer rather than a participant in this world.

Roaming through the crowded school hallways, nodding to her friends, but her mind was elsewhere, consumed with thoughts of perfection and expectations. The assignments piled up, and the pressure to excel felt heavier than ever. She had stayed up late studying, but the exhaustion that clung to her wasn't just from lack of sleep; it was from the nonstop need to be perfect and please everyone around her.

As time crawled by, Meera went through the motions of her daily routine—attending classes, taking notes, and answering questions with the same precision she always did. But something inside her had shifted. She was exhausted—tired of pretending, tired of always pushing herself to meet the expectations that seemed out of reach. And so, in small, almost unnoticeable ways, she began to rebel.

In chemistry class, when the teacher handed out an assignment, Meera detected a spark of rebellion awaken in her. A routine task that she would have usually completed flawlessly, as it was a piece of cake for her—pouring over every detail, ensuring every answer was correct. But this time, she stared at the questions and felt no motivation to give it her all. Instead of thoroughly understanding the material, she carelessly scrawled down responses. They weren't wrong, but they weren't perfect either, and for once, she didn't care. The answers lacked the perfection Meera was always known for, the kind of perfection that used to give her pride, the strength to do it all perfectly. Now, it felt hollow, empty, and pointless. It felt like she was tired of chasing that unreachable standard. For the first time, she didn't care about achieving a flawless score.

No one noticed, of course. Her half-hearted work was still better than most, but to Meera, it felt like a small act of resistance—a way to reclaim some control over her life. It wasn't much, but it was something. She didn't need to be perfect all the time. The weight of meeting every expectation had worn her down, and she was tired of chasing a standard that was never her own.

In literature class, Meera could feel the familiar ache of disappointment—not in the class or her friends, but in herself for refusing to be the star, as she usually shone.

As the teacher posed a question about the poem they were studying, inviting students to share their thoughts, Meera would have eagerly raised her hand normally, but today, she needed space. She didn't raise her hand. She remained silent, allowing another student to take the spotlight. It wasn't that she didn't care about literature anymore; she loved it deeply, but she needed space, and this was her way of taking it.

While having lunch, Meera sat with her friends, but she barely spoke. Their conversation flowed effortlessly as they shared their weekend plans, discussing new movies and upcoming events. Meera listened, her mind swirling with thoughts. Her silence was noticeable to her friends, but they attributed it to pre-exam stress. Low-key, they knew that her silence stemmed from a deeper internal struggle—a battle against the inflexible expectations that had begun to suffocate her.

As the final bell rang, Meera felt a strange sense of calm wash over her. The weight of expectation that had burdened her throughout the day began to lift, if only slightly. But for the first time in a long while, she had pushed back. The small acts of defiance—she pulled in classes by not thinking much before answering questions or not raising her hand, staying quiet—were her way of claiming space. It was as if the sound of the bell had signaled a temporary escape from the pressure to perform flawlessly. The chaos of the school day faded into the background, replaced by a moment of clarity.

Walking home, which didn't feel like home anymore, in the afternoon, Meera's steps felt lighter. She wasn't sure how long she could keep the mask on her face, or how long she could keep up this silent rebellion, or what it would lead to. But for now, it gave her a sense of control over her life—something she had wanted to do for a long time. The streets were filled with the usual sounds, but Meera, deep in her thoughts, wasn't paying attention to that. She was in her own world, contemplating her journey.

Inside her house, the pressure to be perfect still loomed, but today, she had allowed herself a moment of imperfection, a moment to be herself. It wasn't much, but it was enough to keep her going. She had learned that perfection was a burden, not a destination, which weighed heavily on her spirit. The title of being the best was exhausting.

As she settled down to study that evening, Meera realized she would continue to fight her battles alone. But this time, perfection wouldn't dictate her every move. She would embrace her flaws and reclaim her love for learning—one small step at a time.

VII

When Silence Speaks

Meera was exhausted as she sat by the window in her room, watching the rain patter gently against the glass. The rhythm was soothing as she tried to block out the endless voice in her head that constantly whispered the things she still hadn't done—the assignments, exam prep, and the expectations that she hated and at the same time feared the most. Her mind was always spinning, and she felt like she was drowning in her own thoughts. But today, something felt weird in the air, a subtle shift she couldn't figure out.

As she stared out into the rain, trying to block her thoughts, her phone buzzed. She hesitated before picking it up, not wanting to encounter the messages from friends asking about school or plans for the weekend. But when she glanced at the screen, her breath froze; it felt like time had stopped. It wasn't a message from any of her friends—it was from someone she hadn't spoken to in months: Riya, who had been her closest friend. They had been inseparable in middle school, always together and always there for each other. But something had changed in high school. The weight of expectations on Meera made her so focused on studies that she slowly drifted away from Riya. They hadn't fought, just simply grown apart. And now, out of the blue, Riya was reaching out, which shook Meera for a second. Her heart raced as she opened the message:

Hey Meera, I know it's been a while, but I've been thinking about you a lot lately. I miss how we used to be, and I was wondering if you'd want to meet up this weekend. I hope you're doing okay. Let me know.

Meera stared at the message. She hadn't expected this. Part of her was thrilled to hear from Riya again, but another part of her was filled with dread. The walls she had built around herself felt impenetrable, and the thought of letting someone in—even Riya—was terrifying. She had spent so long hiding her struggles, her anxiety, her mental turmoil. Letting Riya back into her life would mean facing those parts of herself that she buried inside.

But even as the anxiety crept in, there was something in Riya's message that tugged at her heart. The simple words "I miss how we used to be" struck a chord. Meera missed it too—missed the carefree days when she didn't feel the need to be perfect all the time, when she had someone who knew her without the mask. Without thinking, her fingers moved, typing out a reply.

I've missed you too. Let's meet.

It was a simple response, but it felt monumental. As she hit send, Meera felt a strange mix of relief and fear. She wasn't sure what this reunion would bring, but for the first time in a long time, she was allowing herself to open up, even if just a little. Riya had seen Meera for who she really was, and maybe—just maybe, with a little bit of hope—she could help Meera find herself again, the way she used to be.

The weekend came faster than she expected. Meera found herself standing outside the café where she and Riya used to meet. Her heart pounded in her chest as she walked through the doors of the café, scanning the room for her friend. And there she was—sitting at a small table near the window, just like old times. Riya looked up, her face breaking into a wide smile as soon as she saw Meera. She waved Meera over.

Meera took a deep breath and walked toward her, each step feeling heavier than the last. But when she sat down, something unexpected happened. The awkwardness she had anticipated wasn't there. Riya's smile was warm and comforting, and the conversation flowed easily, just like old times. They talked about school, about life, for the first time in months. Meera, after a long time, didn't feel the weight of expectations crushing her down.

But then, as they laughed over an old inside joke, Riya suddenly grew serious. She looked Meera in the eyes and said softly, "You know, I've been worried about you."

Meera's heart skipped a beat. It felt like her fear of getting exposed after hiding her struggles, her inner battles, was coming true. "Worried? Why?"

"I don't know," Riya said, her voice gentle. "You just seemed... different. Like you've been carrying something heavy for a long time."

The words hit Meera like a punch to the gut. She wanted to deny it outright, to brush it off with a laugh, but deep inside, she wanted to let all her thoughts out. Meera felt her walls crumbling, felt the truth rising up in her throat. But she swallowed it back down, forcing a smile instead.

"I'm fine," she lied. "Just the usual stress, you know?"

Riya looked unconvinced but decided not to push the conversation further. Instead, she nodded, giving Meera the space she needed. They changed the subject eventually, lightening the stressed atmosphere, and the rest of the afternoon passed in comfortable conversation. But as Meera walked home that evening, her mind was elsewhere, Riya's words echoing in her mind.

She had been worried. She had noticed. Meera wasn't as invisible as she thought.

That night, as Meera lay in bed, staring at the ceiling, sleep long gone, she realized something. She had spent so long fighting her own battles alone, pushing people away, that she had convinced herself no one cared. But Riya had noticed. Riya had reached out. Riya had mentioned it. And maybe, just maybe, she didn't have to fight alone.

But even as she entertained that thought, the little flicker of hope was crushed as Meera knew one thing for sure: She wasn't ready to open up. At least, not yet. The battles she faced were hers to fight. She had survived this long without letting anyone in, and she could for sure survive a little longer.

For now, Meera would keep her mask in place. But the seed of doubt had been planted, and for the first time, she wasn't sure how much longer she could keep fighting this battle on her own.

VIII
Cracks in the Mask

Staring blankly at the textbook in front of her, Meera sat at her desk. The words blurred into an incomprehensible mess as her thoughts drifted elsewhere. The meeting with Riya had stirred something inside her—something unsettling. She thought she had buried her struggles deep enough that no one would notice, but Riya had seen through her. That brief conversation had left her feeling exposed in a way she hadn't anticipated.

The pressure to remain perfect was suffocating; it was killing her from the inside. Her parents still expected top grades, her teachers praised her diligence, and her friends believed she was merely stressed from school. But none of them were able to figure out what was going on inside her mind—except Riya, who had glimpsed beneath the surface. But Meera wasn't ready to break the mask she had worked so hard to perfect. She was convinced and had faith in herself that she could handle everything on her own.

Shaking off her thoughts, just as she began to dive into her studies again, a knock on her door interrupted her. Her mother peeked in, her face a mask of concern.

"Meera, there's a phone call for you," her mother said, holding out the landline.

Meera's heart skipped a beat. No one ever called the landline for her. She grabbed the phone, her mind racing. "Hello?"

"Meera, it's your class teacher," a familiar voice said on the other end. "I wanted to discuss your recent exam results."

Meera's stomach twisted into a knot. Exam results? She had been expecting her scores but hadn't received them yet. "Yes, ma'am?"

"I'm afraid the results are not what we expected from you," her teacher continued, her tone stern but gentle. "Your grades have dropped significantly in the last few tests. Is everything okay?"

The words hit Meera like a punch in the gut. Her grades had dropped? How? She had been working harder than ever—studying late into the night, sacrificing her weekends to stay on top of her studies. She felt a cold sweat break out across her forehead.

"I—I didn't realize, ma'am," Meera stammered. "I've been trying, I really have."

"I can see that, but something seems off," the teacher replied. "You don't seem like yourself in class anymore. I'm worried. If there's anything going on, you can talk to me."

Meera's grip on the phone tightened. Talk? The last thing she wanted to do was open up to a teacher about her personal struggles. She forced a smile into her voice. "Thank you, ma'am. I'll make sure to improve."

Her teacher sighed, as if sensing that Meera wasn't being entirely honest, but she didn't push further. "Alright. Just know that we're here for you if you need anything."

Meera hung up the call, her hands shaking, her mind recalling all the words her teacher had said. The panic that had been lurking beneath the surface now surged to the forefront. How could her grades be slipping when she had been working harder than ever? She had always been the best in class—failure wasn't an option.

But it wasn't just the call that disheartened her. It was what came next.

As she stood up to calm herself, her phone buzzed again—this time, a message from Riya. Meera hesitated for a moment before unlocking the phone.

"Meera, I know you said everything's fine, but I can't shake the feeling that something's wrong. I'm here if you need to talk."

Meera's finger hovered over the screen. She wanted to say something, to tell Riya about the overwhelming pressure, expectations, sleepless nights, and the gnawing anxiety. But she couldn't. Not yet. So instead, she typed:

"I'm fine, Riya. Don't worry about me."

She hit send, but the words felt hollow. She wasn't fine. In fact, she felt like she was slowly unraveling, and she wasn't sure how much longer she could keep it together.

The next morning, the twist that changed everything came unexpectedly.

As Meera made her way to school, her thoughts still preoccupied with the phone call from her teacher, she noticed something strange. Her classmates were whispering as she passed by. People were looking at her, their expressions ranging from confusion to sympathy. Meera's heart pounded in her chest.

When she reached her locker, she saw it—a piece of paper taped to the front. Her stomach dropped as she ripped it off and read the words scrawled in messy handwriting:

"Even the perfect ones fall."

Her breath caught in her throat. She looked around, her mind racing. Who could have written this? How did anyone know about her struggles? Panic clawed at her chest. How could someone know about her internal battles, which she thought she was capable of overcoming by herself? The secret she had been hiding so carefully was starting to slip through the cracks, and she had no idea how to stop it. Meera felt numb.

As the day went on, the whispers grew louder. In class, her classmates glanced at her when she wasn't looking, and by lunchtime, it was clear that something had changed. Someone had spread a rumor about her—about her grades, her slipping up, and the pressure she was under. And worse, the rumor had spread like wildfire.

Meera sat at her usual lunch table with her friends, her mind spinning. She felt exposed, vulnerable, and more alone than ever. It was as if the mask she had worn for so long was finally crumbling. Her fear was coming true, and there was nothing she could do to stop it.

The twist wasn't just the rumor—it was the realization that Meera wasn't as invisible as she thought. People had noticed her struggles, even when she thought she had hidden them so well. The pressure of being perfect had become too much, and now, the cracks were beginning to show.

But Meera wasn't ready to give up. She clenched her fists under the table, her resolve hardening. She would fight this—alone if she had to. She had been through too much to let a few rumors break her.

As the bell rang for the next class, Meera stood up, her head held high. She wasn't going to let anyone see her fall—not yet. The battle was far from over.

"It's the life like one of those,
That I've always feared the most,
When I sit quietly, destroyed.
But through the darkest nights,

I'll find a flicker of light,
A strength within to fight,
And make it through the plight.
Though the pain may never end,
I'll learn to make amends,
And slowly, bit by bit,
I'll learn to live again."

IX

Cracks in the Facade

The weekend was supposed to be a reprieve, but for Meera, it had only amplified the stress. The rumor had spread further than she could have imagined. Her phone was buzzing constantly with messages from her classmates asking if she was okay, if the rumor was true. She had ignored them all. The last thing she wanted was pity or attention.

Sitting at her desk, trying to focus on her studies, but the words on the page seemed to blur. She rubbed her temples, willing herself to concentrate. Her mind, however, was too tangled in the events of the past week. The constant pressure of keeping up the perfect image, combined with the rumor that had shattered her carefully constructed facade, was becoming too much to handle.

She had always been able to handle the pressure—until now. Something about this time felt different. The expectations were heavier, the scrutiny sharper. Meera had always been the reliable one, the one who never slipped, never showed weakness. But now, even her closest friends were asking questions, noticing the change in her demeanor.

Her parents, of course, were oblivious. They saw the same studious, obedient daughter, spending hours at her desk, always pushing herself to excel. They had no idea about the internal storm raging within her. And she intended to keep it that way.

But the cracks in her mask were growing deeper.

That evening, while her parents watched TV in the living room, Meera sat at her desk, staring at her reflection in the mirror. The girl looking back at her seemed like a stranger—someone who was tired and who was barely holding it together. The suffocating weight of expectations, the pressure of being perfect, and the fear of disappointing everyone was choking her. The cracks were no longer subtle—they were glaring.

The girl who was once calm and composed now felt like she was drowning in her own thoughts. She tried to shake it off, convincing herself that she was enough to handle it. But one can't lie to oneself. The truth was that she was exhausted. The relentless study sessions, the sleepless nights, the constant fear of failure—it was all catching up to her.

She sighed, picking up her notebook. It was filled with pages of meticulously written notes, each line perfectly aligned, each word carefully chosen. To anyone else, it would seem like the work of a diligent student. But to Meera, it felt like a prison. Every page reminding her of the pressure she was under, the weight of the expectations that had been placed on her shoulders since childhood.

Her phone buzzed again, pulling her out of her thoughts. It was another message from Riya.

"Meera, I know you're not okay. I'm worried about you. Please talk to me."

Meera stared at the message for a long moment before typing a quick response:

"I'm fine, Riya. Just busy with studies."

It was a lie, of course. But it was easier than admitting the truth—that she was slowly unraveling, that the cracks in her mask were starting to show. She couldn't afford to let anyone in. She had to fight this battle alone, just like she always had.

As the night wore on, Meera continued to work through her assignments, pushing herself harder, determined to maintain the image of the perfect student, the perfect daughter. But deep down, she knew something had to give.

The cracks in her mask were spreading, and no matter how hard she tried to patch them up, they were becoming impossible to hide.

X

Shattered Facade

Monday morning came too quickly. Meera hadn't slept much the night before, her mind racing with the possibilities of the week ahead. As she got ready for school, she moved mechanically, following her usual routine. But today, her hands trembled slightly as she tied her hair into a neat braid and adjusted her uniform. It was as if the calm exterior she had always projected was cracking further with each passing sound.

At school, the whispers were louder than before. She could feel the eyes on her, the stolen glances, the quick conversations that stopped when she passed by. It seemed like everyone knew, or thought they knew, about the rumor. About how the "perfect" Meera had slipped up. The rumor, exaggerated as it traveled, was now something she couldn't control.

She entered her first class, sitting quietly in her seat, trying to ignore the stares. Her friends, though they didn't say it out loud, exchanged concerned glances. Even the teachers seemed to notice the change in her. She could see it in their eyes—the disappointment they tried to hide when her usual enthusiasm seemed to falter, the way they spoke to her more gently, as if they knew something was wrong.

The pressure weighed heavily on her chest, making it hard to breathe. She had always been the strong one, the one who never let anything get to her. But now, it felt like the walls were closing in.

By the time of break, Meera felt drained. Her mind was spinning, and the noise of the cafeteria seemed unbearable. Today, she needed space, so instead of sitting with her friends, pretending to be engaged in their conversations, she made her way to the secluded spot behind the science block—a place she often went to when she needed to be alone. She sat down on the steps, closing her eyes. The air was cooler there. Taking a deep breath, she hoped for a moment of peace.

But peace never came.

Her phone buzzed in her pocket, indicating another message. She didn't need to check to know it was Riya again, probably asking her to talk, to open up. Meera didn't reply. She couldn't. The idea of talking about what she was going through felt like admitting defeat, like acknowledging that she couldn't handle it. But the truth was, she couldn't handle it anymore.

A tear slipped down her cheek, surprising her. She hadn't cried in so long; she had almost forgotten what it felt like. Another tear followed, and before she knew it, she was sobbing quietly, the weight of everything crashing down on her. All the pressure, the expectations, the rumor—it was too much.

For the first time in decades, Meera allowed herself to feel the full weight of her pain. She had always been so focused on being strong, on keeping it together, that she had forgotten what it felt like to break.

But even as the tears fell, something inside her hardened. This had to stop. She couldn't keep living like this—constantly trying to meet everyone else's expectations, sacrificing her own happiness for an image that wasn't even real. She had been trying so hard to be the perfect daughter, the perfect student, that she had lost sight of herself.

The crying stopped as suddenly as it had begun. Meera wiped her eyes, staring at the empty lunchbox in front of her. She wasn't done yet. This wasn't the end.

But things needed to change. If she couldn't meet everyone's expectations, she would focus on her own. If people wanted to talk, let them. It was too bad if they expected her to be perfect; it was their loss, their mistake.

She stood up, feeling strangely lighter. Her heart still hurt, but now there was a determination in her that hadn't been there before. She wasn't going to let this pressure consume her. She didn't need to be perfect. She just needed to survive. And if that meant fighting her battles in silence, then so be it.

As she made her way back to class, Meera felt something new: a quiet, unspoken determination. She wasn't going to let the world break her. Not today.

XI

The Calm After the Storm

The next day, Meera woke up before dawn, the early morning light barely seeping through her bedroom window. The air was cold, and the stillness of the house matched the quiet determination that had settled in her heart. It was a strange kind of peace, the calm that follows a storm.

As she got ready for school, her movements were steady. There was no rush, no frantic need to look perfect. Her hair was tied into a simple ponytail, and her uniform was neatly ironed, but she didn't care for perfection anymore. She wasn't trying to hide behind a polished image today. Today, she would simply be Meera, who had accepted all her flaws and struggles.

At breakfast, her parents barely noticed the shift in her demeanor. Her mother talked about the weekend's plans, her father continued the conversation with some work issues, and Meera nodded along, the way she always did.

But inside, something had changed. She was no longer weighed down by their expectations. She knew they meant well, but they didn't see her—the real her, with all her flaws and struggles. They only saw the version of her that they had created, the one she had worked hard to maintain.

When she reached school, her friends greeted her with their usual energy, but she could tell that they were still concerned. Riya, especially, kept looking at her with worry in her eyes, but Meera smiled reassuringly, keeping the conversation light.

"Are you okay, Meera? You seem...uh, distant lately," Riya asked slowly when they were alone, her eyes full of concern.

Meera paused for a moment, the question hanging in the air. For a split second, she considered telling Riya the truth—about the suffocating pressure, the sleepless nights, and the tears she had cried alone. But then she shook her head.

"I'm fine," she said, her voice steady. "Just tired from studying, you know how it is."

Riya nodded, accepting the answer, though Meera could tell she wasn't fully convinced. But that was the thing about Meera—she had become an expert at pretending. Pretending to be okay, pretending to have it all together, pretending that the weight on her shoulders wasn't crushing her.

As the day went on, Meera stuck to her resolve. In class, she focused on the lessons, taking notes diligently, but not obsessing over every detail like she used to. When her math teacher handed back the latest test, her heart didn't race like it usually did. She got an 85—far from the perfect score she usually received—but it didn't bother her. Not anymore.

She wasn't trying to be perfect, to be what everyone around her wanted her to be. She was trying to survive.

At lunch, Meera joined her friends again, but this time she didn't feel the need to force herself into their conversations. She listened quietly, nodding when appropriate, but her mind was elsewhere. She could tell that they noticed the change in her, but no one pressed the issue. They were used to the old Meera—the one who always had a bright smile and a quick response—a chatterbox. The girl who seemed to have everything under control.

But this new version of herself—the quieter, more contemplative Meera—felt more real. She was done pretending to be something she wasn't.

The rumors at school were floating around, but Meera didn't seem to care anymore. She had spent too much time worrying about what other people thought, trying to live up to an image that wasn't hers to begin with. Let them talk. Let them think what they wanted. She knew her truth.

That afternoon, as she walked home from school, Meera felt lighter than she had in months. The sky was overcast, and a light drizzle began to fall, but she didn't mind. The cool rain against her skin was refreshing, washing away the remnants of her old self.

As she reached her front door, she paused for a moment, taking in the familiar sight of her home. This was the place where she had learned to be perfect, where she had crafted her mask. But now, she wasn't hiding anymore.

Stepping inside, she greeted her parents with a small smile, then headed to her room. The weight of their expectation was still there, lingering in the background, but it no longer had the power to crush her. She had fought her way through the darkness, and though the battles weren't over, she now knew she could face them.

That evening, as she sat by her desk, Meera picked up her notebook and began writing again. The words flowed easily, without hesitation or fear. For the first time in a long while, she wasn't writing for anyone else. She wasn't trying to prove anything. She was writing for herself.

And that, she realized, was enough.

For the first time in a long while, Meera felt a small spark of hope flicker within her.

XII
Behind the Mask

It was an ordinary day. Meera had gone through the motions as usual—waking up, attending classes, listening to her teachers. She had been quiet, as always, and by now, her friends had stopped asking if she was okay. They had accepted her silence, attributing it to the endless grind of academics and the pressures of school life. But today, something felt different.

During lunch, Riya came over and sat next to Meera, pulling out her phone. She scrolled through social media, casually showing Meera some pictures from the school's annual festival that had just been uploaded. Meera half-listened, her mind elsewhere, until a particular image caught her attention. It was a photo of her—standing alone near the science exhibition booth—staring blankly ahead, with dark circles under her eyes and an expression that screamed exhaustion.

"Look at this," Riya chuckled softly, but there was a hint of concern in her voice. "You look so lost here, Meera. Are you sure you're alright?"

Meera glanced at the photo again, feeling a sudden surge

of discomfort. The girl in the picture looked so different from the person she had been trying to present. It was like seeing her raw emotions captured in a single snapshot, and it frightened her. She mumbled something in response, brushing it off as a bad angle, but the truth was, it hit her harder than she wanted to admit.

Later, in the privacy of her bedroom, Meera stared at the photo again. It had already started circulating on social media, and people had commented—most of them playful jokes about her looking *"zoned out"* or *"deep in thought."* But some of the comments weren't so lighthearted.

"She always looks tired, like she's carrying the world on her shoulders."

"Is Meera okay? She used to be so cheerful."

"I think she's just stressed out. All those grades are finally getting to her."

Meera's chest tightened as she read the comments. For the first time, it felt like people were seeing through her mask, noticing the cracks in her perfect image. Her fingers trembled as she scrolled through more pictures, all of them showcasing her classmates enjoying themselves, laughing, and carefree. She, on the other hand, looked detached—isolated even in a crowd.

Just as she was about to put her phone away, a message popped up from an unknown number. Her heart skipped a beat as she opened it.

"Hey, Meera. I've been wanting to talk to you for a while. You seem... different. Is everything okay? Don't worry, I won't tell anyone, but if you need to talk, I'm here."

She stared at the message, the words blurring as panic gripped her. Who was this? How had they noticed? For a moment, Meera considered replying, but then something inside her snapped. The idea of confiding in someone, even anonymously, felt wrong. She didn't want pity, didn't want anyone to see her weakness. She couldn't afford to let anyone in.

Instead of responding, she deleted the message.

The next day, as Meera walked into school, she couldn't shake the feeling that everyone was watching her. Whispers seemed to follow her wherever she went, and though no one said anything directly, she could feel the weight of their eyes on her. Her mind raced with thoughts about the message. Was there a rumor going around about her?

During science class, her worst fear came true. The teacher had assigned a group project, and as they divided into teams, Meera found herself paired with a boy named Aaryan. He was quiet and observant, the type who never spoke unless he had something important to say. As they sat together, working on their experiment, he glanced at her, his expression unreadable.

"You've changed lately, you know," Aaryan said softly, not looking up from the beaker in front of him. "You're not the same Meera from last year."

Meera's breath caught in her throat. She didn't know how to respond to this, so she kept quiet, hoping he would drop the subject.

"I don't mean to pry," he continued, "but you're not fooling anyone with that smile. You don't have to pretend."

Her stomach churned with unease. Aaryan's words were like a knife, cutting through the careful façade she had built. How could he see so clearly through her when she had spent so long perfecting her mask? She hadn't realized that her struggle had become so visible.

She wanted to lash out, to tell him he didn't know anything about her life, but the truth was, he had hit a nerve. Her silence stretched on, the tension between them growing thick. Finally, Aaryan sighed and went back to focusing on the experiment.

For the rest of the day, Meera couldn't concentrate. Aaryan's words haunted her, replaying over and over in her mind. Had everyone been able to see through her all along? Was she that obvious? That transparent? The thought terrified her.

When she got home, she did something she hadn't done in a long time—she sat down at her desk and opened her notebook. The one where she used to write her poetry. But instead of the usual verses, she scribbled words furiously, as if trying to purge the overwhelming emotions that had been building up inside her.

"Perfection is a lie," she wrote. *"A mask we wear to hide our fear, our pain, our brokenness. But the cracks are showing, and no one can pretend forever."*

As she wrote, something in her shifted. The weight of the expectations, the pressure to be flawless—it had all been building to this moment. And in that moment, she realized something she had been avoiding for so long: she didn't want to be perfect anymore.

The next day at school, Meera made a decision. She wasn't going to pretend anymore. She wasn't going to be the perfect daughter, the perfect student, or the perfect friend. She was just going to be herself—flawed, struggling, and human.

And as she walked into class, for the first time, she didn't care who was watching.

XIII

Shattered Control

Meera walked into the school library, hoping to find a quiet place where she could think. The last few days had been overwhelming, with Aaryan's words still echoing in her mind. No matter how much she tried to push them away, they lingered, gnawing at her sense of control.

She slid into a chair in the corner of the library, away from the few students who were scattered across the room. Her notebook, open in front of her, displayed the half-finished scribbles from the day before, staring back at her. But today, the words wouldn't come. Her mind was too clouded, too full of anxiety.

For years, she had prided herself on being in control of everything—her emotions, her grades, her image. She had perfected the art of juggling everyone's expectations without letting anyone see how much it was tearing her apart. But now, it felt like the walls she had so carefully constructed were closing in on her. She felt trapped in her own life.

Suddenly, her phone buzzed with a message. It was from her mom, reminding her to come home early and finish studying for her upcoming exams. Meera sighed, the pressure building once again. Everyone around her kept reminding her of what she had to do, what she had to be, as if her entire worth was tied to her performance in school.

Closing her notebook, she decided to leave the library. She couldn't focus here, and the thought of studying was suffocating. She needed air. It was getting hard for her to breathe under all the pressure.

Outside, the cool breeze brushed against her face as Meera walked, her feet taking her to a park near her house. She hadn't been here in a long time—maybe because it was a place that reminded her of her childhood, when things had been simpler. Back then, when there were no expectations, no pressure of being perfect, no fake smiles, no masks. Back then, when she could just be herself.

Sitting on a park bench, Meera closed her eyes and tried to calm her racing thoughts. But instead of peace, her mind was flooded with memories—memories of her parents pushing her to excel, her teachers praising her for being the model student, her friends looking up to her as if she had all the answers. The title of "PERFECT."

But the truth was, Meera didn't have the answers. She was just as lost as everyone else. Maybe even more than them.

Meera felt a pang of jealousy when the familiar sound of laughter pulled her out of her thoughts. A group of kids were playing nearby, chasing each other and shouting with joy. The carefree laughter echoed in the air. She missed that feeling—the freedom to be carefree, to be happy without the weight of everyone around her on her shoulders.

As she watched the children play, she realized something: she didn't know who she was without the expectations. Her entire identity had been built around being the perfect daughter, the perfect student. But without those things, who was she?

The thought scared her. It felt like she was standing on the edge of a cliff, staring into an abyss. She had spent so long trying to be in control of everything that now, when things were slipping out of her grasp, she didn't know how to handle it.

Meera looked down at her trembling hands. She clenched them into fists, trying to steady herself. She couldn't let things fall apart. She had to keep going, had to maintain control.

But deep down, she knew it was only a matter of time before she couldn't hold on any longer.

The next day, Meera returned to school with a forced sense of calm. She walked into class, sat in her usual seat, and took out her books. But today felt different. The weight of her internal struggle was becoming unbearable, and no matter how hard she tried to push it down, it was seeping into every part of her life.

As the teacher started teaching, Meera found herself zoning out. Her eyes scanned the board, but the words didn't register. Her mind was somewhere else—lost in a swirl of anxiety and doubt that had been consuming her.

Suddenly, the teacher called her name, pulling her out of her thoughts. "Meera, can you answer this question?"

Meera snapped back to reality, her heart racing. She hadn't been paying attention, and now, all eyes were on her. She fumbled for an answer, her voice shaky and unsure. But before she could finish, the teacher moved on, sensing that something was off.

The rest of the class passed in a blur, and by the time the bell rang, Meera felt like she was on the verge of a breakdown. She hurried out of the classroom, trying to escape the growing sense of panic that was threatening to overwhelm her.

Outside, she found a secluded spot near the school's garden and sat down on a bench, her hands trembling once again. This time, the calm she had felt after Aaryan's confrontation was gone. Instead, she was spiraling, losing her grip on the carefully crafted control she had maintained for so long.

In that moment, Meera realized something terrifying: she was no longer in control. The weight of perfection, the endless expectations, and the internal battle she had been fighting were finally catching up to her.

For the first time in her life, she didn't know how to keep going.

XIV
Cracks in the Armor

Meera walked into class that morning, but an unsettling energy lingered in the air. As she slid into her seat, she noticed the glances from her classmates—quick and tinged with something she couldn't quite place. Whispers filled the corners of the room, quiet enough to be almost silent yet loud enough to unsettle her.

She reached for her notebook, hoping the feel of the pages would calm her, but before she could open it, Divya, her closest friend, leaned over. "Meera," she whispered urgently, glancing around before she spoke. "Did you... did you hear what happened?"

Meera shook her head slowly, her heart pounding, sensing something was off. Divya hesitated, clearly struggling to find the right words. "Someone shared the class scores online last night," she said, barely audible. "Not just names and grades, but details about who's falling behind, who's been struggling... everything. Everyone's talking about it."

Anxiety prickled down Meera's spine as Divya's words sank in. This was more than just a rumor; it was an invasion, and she feared her own struggles might be on display. She'd tried so hard to keep up, to shield her slipping grades from everyone around her, but everything had gone in vain. Now, the veil of her carefully constructed life felt paper-thin.

Trying to calm herself, Meera scanned the room, locking eyes with the students she barely knew. She could sense them seeing through her, witnessing the cracks she'd worked so hard to hide. The walls she had built to protect herself were now crumbling, one whisper at a time.

During lunch, she sat alone in her usual corner, feeling the weight of betrayal crush her. Now, she felt exposed and vulnerable. She caught Divya's gaze from across the courtyard, full of pity.

In the days that followed, Meera retreated even further into herself, finding solace only in the pages of her notebook, where she poured out her feelings in the form of poetry—her only peace. Each verse was a testament to her struggle, to her battles, to the endless pressure she bore, yet she knew it was no longer enough to hold back everything.

"They first notice my scars,
Then ask me how you are?
The one who notices my dark circles,
Asking me what I'm doing all day?
The one who catches my silent tears,
Questioning if I've faced my fears.
They notice the tremor in my voice,
Asking if sorrow was my choice.
They observe the burden on my soul,
Asking if I've lost control.

The one who senses my silent fight,
Wondering if I'll be alright."

The twist had fractured something fundamental inside her—a trust she had placed in her own resilience. And as the days wore on, Meera found herself grappling with an unsettling question: What happens when even the strongest armor starts to crack?

Her mask was slipping, and the world around her was watching closely, waiting to see if she could hold it all together.

XV
Letters to Nowhere

Days blurred together as Meera sank deeper into herself, her world dimming under the weight of expectation and isolation. She went through the motions—attending classes, nodding when spoken to, answering questions mechanically—but inside, she felt distant, as if a glass wall separated her from everyone else. The only thing that brought her solace now was her poetry notebook, hidden like a treasure beneath her schoolbooks. Each night, she poured her thoughts onto the page, scribbling down verses, emotions, and secrets she dared not spill out to anyone.

One evening, after a particularly exhausting day at school, Meera found herself drawn to an old wooden box on her desk—the box where she kept letters she'd never sent. It was a habit she'd started in middle school, a way to cope with emotions she couldn't express. These letters had never seen the light of day, yet each one held a piece of her heart.

On impulse, she pulled out a fresh sheet of paper and began writing a new letter, one meant for no one in particular but filled with the raw honesty she kept hidden.

Dear Someone,

I don't know who you are or if you'll ever read this, but writing feels like therapy, the only way to breathe right now. Everything feels wrong; it sucks. My days feel like endless returns of a life that doesn't belong to me. It's getting hard to exist even. Each morning, I put on this mask, smile, act as if everything is okay. And no one knows that inside, I feel like I'm standing on the edge of a cliff, barely holding on. Life, this is not how I wanted it to be.

I'm not even sure who I am anymore. Everyone around me has this perfect picture of who I'm supposed to be—Mom's "good girl," Dad's "future doctor." But no one asks me what I want. They tell me what I need to become. And I... I'm just tired. I feel like a puzzle forced into the wrong frame.

Sometimes I think about running away, finding a place where I can start over without these expectations crushing me. But I don't think I'd even know how to be that version of me. What if this mask is all I have left? What if I take it off and find nothing underneath?

I hope, somehow, someday, I find a way to breathe without feeling so heavy inside.

Love,

Me

୨୭

As she finished the letter, her hand trembled, and she felt tears prickling her eyes. She hadn't cried in a long time, holding everything in for so long that the release felt both freeing and terrifying. She folded the letter carefully, slipping it into the box with the others. It felt safer there, locked away where no one would ever see it.

The next day, Meera walked into school feeling a strange sense of relief. The weight of her emotions felt lighter, as if confiding them, even just on paper, had loosened the iron grip around her heart. She noticed details she'd ignored before—the sound of laughter from a group of friends, the smell of flowers blooming. There was a glimmer of beauty around her, which she hadn't seen in a long time. It felt like the world was offering her moments of solace she'd been too weighed down to notice.

At lunch, she wandered over to the school's small library. It was quiet, with only a few students sitting at the table, engrossed in their books. She found a secluded corner near the back, away from everyone else, and opened her poetry notebook. Her mind raced with thoughts, images, and fragments of verses, all begging to be put into words.

But as she flipped through the pages, her eyes fell on a bookmark tucked inside, one she hadn't noticed before. It wasn't hers. Curious, she pulled it out and read the words scrawled on it in messy, uneven handwriting:

"One day, you'll look back and realize these struggles shaped the person you were meant to become. Keep going."

The words struck her deeply, as if they'd been written just for her. She looked around the library, hoping to find someone watching her, but she was alone. The message felt like a gift—an unexpected reassurance that someone, somewhere in this world, understood the pain, even though she had no idea who it was.

The note became her secret treasure, a reminder she could return to when things felt too heavy to cope. Tucking it safely into her notebook, she closed her eyes for a moment. For the first time in a long while, she felt the beginnings of hope. Perhaps, she thought, maybe—just maybe—she could find her way through the darkness after all.

XVI
Threads of Connection

She'd revisit the words during difficult moments, drawing strength from them. It was strange, she thought in the days that followed, how a few words scribbled on a piece of paper could bring her a sense of calm that no amount of academic praise or encouragement from family had ever managed to.

In the days that followed, Meera carried the note with her, tucked safely in her poetry notebook.

One afternoon, while in the library, Meera decided to do something she had never done before. She opened her notebook and wrote her own small note:

"For anyone who feels lost: I know the struggle. Keep going. You're stronger than you think."

She tore the page out and slipped it between the pages of a random book on the shelf, hoping that someone, someday, would find it and feel the same comfort she had.

She began leaving little messages like that in hidden corners of the school—at the back of her desk, taped inside her locker, even behind a poster in the hallway. Each note was different, but they all carried words of encouragement, reminders of resilience, and a promise that struggle was temporary. She didn't know who would find them or if they would resonate with anyone, but the act of leaving them brought her quiet satisfaction.

One day, Meera noticed a new note slipped under the door of her locker. It was scrawled in familiar handwriting, as if the person who had left the original bookmark had seen her messages and responded.

"I know your heart, the way you carry it alone. Thank you. Keep going."

The words felt like a direct connection to someone out there—a stranger who somehow understood her silent struggle and her small acts of kindness. The exchange became a silent conversation between her and this unknown friend. It was unspoken, unseen, yet strangely comforting. Through these notes, she felt a sense of belonging she hadn't felt in a long time.

From that day on, Meera carried a quiet strength within her. She still felt the pressure of her responsibilities, the weight of her family's expectations, and the burden of perfection, but there was a shift. The notes reminded her that she wasn't as alone as she had once believed.

By the time the year was halfway over, she had begun to notice the same faces in the library every day—a boy always reading science fiction novels, a girl sketching quietly in the corner, a group of friends laughing together over their textbooks. She began to feel a sense of kinship, recognizing that maybe everyone was struggling in their own ways, carrying battles no one could see.

And perhaps, just perhaps, someone was looking out for her, in a way she couldn't explain. It gave her the courage to keep moving forward, one step at a time.

XVII

Unseen Battles

The next morning, Meera arrived at school with a sense of quiet resolve she hadn't felt before. The act of writing those anonymous notes had awakened something within her—a hidden strength she hadn't realized she possessed. She had spent so long feeling isolated by her struggles, but now, knowing that her small words of encouragement might be helping someone else gave her a new sense of purpose. In a way, it healed parts of her that had never been comforted.

As she walked into her first class, she noticed an unexpected note tucked beneath her textbook. The sight of it sent a rush of anticipation through her. She carefully unfolded it, her hands trembling slightly. It read:

"Your words mean more than you know. They helped me through a dark day. Thank you."

She read it again, warmth spreading through her chest. Somewhere, someone had needed those words as much as she had. Somehow, they had reached each other. Her heart swelled with the realization that, perhaps, by giving others hope, she was finding her own.

The day carried on as usual, but Meera's thoughts lingered on the unknown person who had left her the note. She wondered who it could be—someone in her classes, one of the many students she passed in the halls, or maybe even someone she'd never met. The idea felt comforting, like a quiet reminder that connection didn't always require knowing someone's face or voice.

At lunch, she felt compelled to do something a bit bolder. She wrote another note, longer this time, and made her way to the library. In careful, neat handwriting, she wrote:

"For whoever finds this: You are seen. You are heard. You're not alone, even when it feels like it. Life isn't like a movie with happy endings. It can be hard, but there's beauty in every struggle. We'll get through this together. Keep going."

She tucked the note inside a well-worn novel on the top shelf and stepped back, feeling a familiar rush of adrenaline. This time, though, she wasn't just thinking about helping someone else. She was also helping herself.

Later that week, Meera sat in the library again, poring over a textbook but struggling to focus. She watched the other students around her and, for the first time, felt more observant, more curious. She noticed the little things—the way some people tapped their pencils when they were nervous or how others sat quietly, lost in their own thoughts. Everyone had their own stories, their own silent battles. And she began to wonder if maybe, just maybe, they were all part of a quiet network, each unknowingly giving one another courage just by existing in the same space.

Then, something caught her eye. A piece of paper was folded and taped under the library table where she always sat. Her heart raced as she reached for it. It read:

"We're stronger than we know. Keep fighting. Keep hoping."

She smiled, realizing her anonymous friend was still out there, leaving words of comfort and hope for her to find. This time, she didn't feel alone in her battle. She had an ally, even if they'd never met face-to-face. For the first time, she felt like she was sharing the weight of her burdens, as though someone had lifted a part of her struggle off her shoulders.

The days continued, each one bringing a new challenge but also a new note—a fresh reminder that someone out there was rooting for her. She wasn't alone in her silent battle. The notes became her own private messages of hope, tucked away in hidden places she discovered by chance. They reminded her of her strength and resilience, echoing the sentiment that she was not as alone as she had once felt.

By the end of the week, Meera felt inspired to create something of her own—a small poetry collection, dedicated to everyone who struggles in silence. She spent her evenings crafting verses that poured from her heart, words she wished someone had said to her, words she hoped could resonate with others the way those notes had resonated with her. She titled it "Unseen Battles." It was her way of expressing the emotions she kept hidden—a tribute to the silent warriors like her who fought their battles alone.

With each poem, she felt her heart lighten a bit, as if releasing her emotions onto paper allowed her to breathe a little easier. She didn't tell anyone about it, not even her friends. This was something private, a piece of her soul shared only with the pages that could carry the weight of her unspoken thoughts.

As she finished the final poem, she felt a profound sense of calm—a peace that had been elusive for so long. She didn't know if anyone would ever read her words, but that didn't matter. She had created something that expressed the struggles she'd held within her for so long, and it had brought her a new sense of closure.

On the last page of her collection, she wrote:

"To those who fight in silence: Know that you are never truly alone. There is strength in your battle and beauty in your resilience. Keep going."

She closed the notebook, holding it close to her chest, feeling warmth she hadn't felt in years.

XVIII

The Strength in Silence

The next day, Meera walked into school with a subtle but undeniable change in her demeanor. She felt lighter, as if writing her poetry collection, Unseen Battles, had unlocked a hidden strength within her. The sense of isolation that had weighed her down for so long seemed to fade. Her words, quietly poured onto paper, had given her newfound clarity and calm.

As she walked through the halls, Meera noticed things she hadn't before. She observed the faces around her, each one lost in its own world, and realized that everyone carried hidden stories. That realization made her feel less alone.

In her literature class, Mrs. Vedi introduced an upcoming school project involving "creative expression." The students could choose any medium—art, music, writing, or performance—to convey a personal experience or message. As Mrs. Vedi explained the details, Meera felt a spark of inspiration. She had never considered sharing her poetry publicly, but maybe... just maybe, this was her chance to let others see a glimpse of her inner world.

After class, Mrs. Vedi caught up with Meera. "I see a change in you, Meera," she said with a gentle smile. "It's as though you've found something to hold onto."

Meera hesitated before responding. "I think... I think I've found a way to express things I couldn't say out loud." She didn't go into detail, but Mrs. Vedi's knowing nod made her feel understood.

The rest of the day passed in a blur as Meera's thoughts focused on how to bring her poems to life for the project. At lunch, she returned to the library, her safe haven. She pulled out her notebook and flipped through *Unseen Battles*, rereading the words she had written. Each poem felt like a piece of her soul, and she knew that sharing them would mean exposing a vulnerable part of herself.

Just then, she noticed a small note tucked between the books on the shelf in front of her. With a sense of anticipation, her heart beating a little faster, she reached for it. The note read:

"Your courage inspires others. Thank you for reminding me that we're stronger than our silence."

Meera's heart swelled with emotion. She had no idea who was leaving these messages, but each one felt like a small reminder that her quiet efforts weren't going unnoticed. Someone, somewhere, was seeing her words and finding comfort in them, just as she had found solace in theirs.

That evening, Meera stayed up late working on her project. She carefully selected the poems from *Unseen Battles* that resonated most with her journey—the ones that captured her silent struggles and the strength she had found within. She decided to create a small, hand-bound book of her poems, dedicating it to *"the unseen warriors" as a tribute to everyone who, like her, fought their battles in silence.*

On the day of the project presentations, Meera's heart raced as she approached the front of the class, holding her poetry collection. She took a deep breath before speaking, feeling the weight of vulnerability in each word.

"This... this is called *Unseen Battles*," she began, her voice steady but soft. "It's a collection of poems I wrote as a way to understand my own struggles and to remind myself—and hopefully others—that even in silence, there's strength."

As she read her poems aloud, a hush fell over the room. Her words filled the space, weaving a story of resilience, quiet battles, and hidden strength. For the first time, Meera felt truly seen. Her voice resonated in a way she had never imagined.

When she finished, there was a moment of silence before her classmates began to clap, some with tears in their eyes, offering her looks of admiration.

Mrs. Vedi approached her afterward, her eyes filled with pride. "You have a gift, Meera. Thank you for sharing it with us."

As Meera left the class, several classmates came up to her, sharing their own stories and telling her how her words had made them feel understood. She was overwhelmed, yet grateful. She had taken a step she never thought she could, and in doing so, she had touched others in ways she couldn't have imagined.

That night, she added one final poem to Unseen Battles:

"What if this all is a lie, this all is a bad dream,
What if there is no helplessness, no muffled scream?
What if people don't scuffle, don't fall,
What if there's love everywhere, and no tear at all?
What if there's a dawn after every dark night,

What if within every struggle, there's a chance for light?
What if beyond every shadow, there's a radiant sun,
What if after all the battles, peace can still be won?"

She closed the book, holding it close to her chest, feeling a warmth she hadn't felt in years. She had discovered that her silence held strength, her words held power, and her journey, though challenging, had led her to a place of quiet courage she could carry with her always.

XIX

The Ripple Effect

The day after her presentation, Meera walked into school feeling more grounded than ever. There was a calm resolve within her, a sense that she hadn't just allowed others to see her struggles but had embraced her own journey with a strength she hadn't realized existed. Her poems had sparked something—she could see it in the warm smiles and greetings of her classmates.

At lunch, her friend Riya sat down beside her. She hesitated before speaking, her fingers nervously tracing patterns on the table.

"Meera... I never knew you were going through so much. You always seem so composed, like you have everything together," she said softly. "Hearing your poems made me realize... we're all dealing with things, even if no one sees it."

Meera smiled, her gaze gentle and reassuring. "We all wear masks, don't we? We pretend we're fine until it gets too hard to hide anymore. Sometimes... it's okay to let someone see behind it."

Riya nodded, and after a brief silence, she began sharing bits of her own struggles—her worries about living up to her parents' high expectations, the pressure to always excel, and the fear of letting people down. As Riya spoke, it was as if a dam had burst. One by one, Meera's friends started sharing their own stories.

Meera was surprised by how much they were all carrying beneath their bright smiles. The group sat there for a long time, peeling back the layers they hadn't even realized they'd been hiding. Meera felt a quiet pride, knowing that by sharing her own struggles, she had given her friends permission to confront theirs.

Later, as Meera turned away from the bulletin board in the hallway, she ran into a familiar face—Mrs. Rao. Her teacher smiled knowingly, her eyes soft with understanding.

"You've done more than you realize, Meera," she said. "You haven't just shared your story; you've given others the courage to share theirs."

Meera felt her cheeks flush with gratitude. "Thank you, Mrs. Rao. I never imagined it would mean so much to everyone."

"That's the thing about courage," Mrs. Rao replied. "It's contagious."

As Meera walked away, her thoughts drifted to the notes she had hidden, the words she had written, and the way those words had taken on a life of their own. She wondered how far they might travel, how many lives they might touch. For the first time, she felt like she was part of something bigger—a quiet movement of connection and understanding.

That night, sitting at her desk, Meera opened her poetry notebook. The words came easily, spilling onto the page as though they had been waiting for her:

"A quiet whisper, a gentle hand,
We lift each other where we stand.
A ripple of kindness, a spark of light,
Together we rise, through every fight."

As she finished, Meera smiled to herself, feeling a peace she hadn't known before. She wasn't alone anymore. Her struggles might still come and go, but she now understood the power of connection—that even the smallest gestures could create ripples of hope and strength

XX
Threads of Resilience

The weeks that followed were a whirlwind for Meera. She was both surprised and humbled by how her small acts of kindness had resonated so deeply with others. Her words, once scattered across the campus in hidden notes and whispered in fleeting conversations, had sparked a quiet revolution in her school.

Everywhere she looked, there were signs of change. New friendships formed, classmates exchanged words of encouragement, and even a simple nod or smile carried the unspoken message: *I understand.*

One morning, as she walked down the hallway, her attention was drawn to the bulletin board. What had once been a blank space was now a vibrant collage of colorful notes. Some were brief—*"Don't give up."* Others were more personal, sharing pieces of struggles and gratitude for the mysterious notes that had started it all. Meera felt an overwhelming mix of pride and disbelief that something so small could mean so much to so many.

During lunch, she wandered to her usual quiet spot near the library. Her friends had noticed a shift in her. Her smiles lingered longer, her laughter felt lighter, and there was a sense of calm about her. Yet, Meera still kept her deepest struggles to herself. This journey of healing was deeply personal, and she needed to navigate it on her own terms.

Sitting in the library, she opened her poetry notebook to a blank page. Words began to flow effortlessly, inspired by the strength she had found in herself and the unseen connections she had made with others:

"We are woven from threads unseen,
Bound by battles never spoken,
A quiet courage, steady and keen,
In broken words, resilience awoken."

The words felt like a balm to her soul. Writing had become her sanctuary—a space where she could be honest without fear of judgment. She wasn't sure what she would do with these poems someday. Perhaps she'd share them, or maybe they'd remain tucked away in this worn notebook. For now, they were her lifeline.

Her thoughts were interrupted by the sound of footsteps. She looked up to see Priya, one of her classmates, standing nearby with a hesitant smile.

"Mind if I sit?" Priya asked, gesturing to the empty seat beside her.

"Of course," Meera replied, surprised. Priya wasn't someone she had been particularly close to, but she welcomed the company.

They sat in silence for a moment before Priya spoke, her voice uncertain. "I know you've been... leaving those notes around the school," she began, glancing at Meera. "I don't know if you wanted people to figure it out, but... I knew it was you. You've always had a way with words."

Meera flushed, caught off guard. "I didn't think anyone would guess," she admitted, a small smile tugging at her lips. "I just wanted to help."

Priya nodded, her expression softening. "You did. More than you know. Those notes... they really helped me. I was going through so much, and I didn't know how to talk to anyone about it. But reading those words, knowing someone cared... it made a difference."

Meera reached over, her hand resting lightly on Priya's arm. "I'm glad they helped," she said gently. "Sometimes, just knowing you're not alone can mean everything."

What followed was an open conversation—one that neither of them had expected. Priya spoke about her struggles at home, the weight of family expectations, and the loneliness that came with feeling invisible. Meera, in turn, shared her own battles with perfectionism, the pressure to excel, and the yearning to be seen for more than her achievements.

By the time they parted, Meera felt a new sense of kinship with Priya, a bond forged in shared vulnerability. It reminded her that even the smallest gestures could create ripples of understanding and connection.

In the days that followed, Meera noticed subtle changes in herself. She felt lighter, as though the weight she had been carrying had eased just enough for her to breathe more freely. There were still moments of doubt, days when the pressure felt overwhelming. But in those moments, she turned to her poetry, letting her words transform pain into something meaningful.

One evening, inspired by the events of the past weeks, Meera decided to compile her poems into a small book. She titled it Threads of Resilience—a tribute to the invisible bonds that connected her to her classmates, her friends, and even to strangers who might find solace in her words.

On the first page, she wrote a dedication:
"For those who fight in silence,
For the warriors unseen,
May you find courage in these words,
And know you are not alone."

The act of writing those words felt like a release, a way of letting go of the pain she had carried for so long. She felt at peace, knowing that her experiences had a purpose.

The following Monday, Meera brought her completed collection to school. She placed it in the library's donation box, unsure if anyone would ever read it. But the thought that her words might comfort someone, might make them feel less alone, filled her with quiet satisfaction.

As she left the library, she glanced at the bulletin board. A fresh wave of notes had appeared, each one brimming with resilience and compassion. One, in particular, caught her eye:
"We are stronger than we think, braver than we know.
Thank you to whoever started this. You made us all feel seen."

Meera smiled, her heart swelling with gratitude. She realized then that her journey had never been solely about her own healing. It was about creating a space where others could find strength and hope, where they could feel understood.

As she walked down the hallway, she felt the warmth of those invisible threads—binding her to everyone around her, weaving a tapestry of resilience, compassion, and quiet courage. She knew there would still be challenges ahead, but she was ready to face them.

Because now, she understood that healing was not just a solitary path—it was a collective one. Together, they were stronger.

XXI

Unseen Bonds

As winter cast its serene stillness over the town, Meera found herself experiencing an unfamiliar calm, one that resonated deeply within her. The school, once teetering on the edge of indifference, had transformed into a hub of warmth and connection. The anonymous notes that had sparked this quiet revolution now covered the bulletin board, spilling onto nearby walls in a cascade of colors. Everywhere she turned, she saw her classmates leaning on one another for support, exchanging genuine smiles, and sharing silent nods of understanding.

One frosty morning, as students shuffled out of her literature class, Mrs. Kapoor, her teacher, called Meera over. A pang of nervousness hit her—she wasn't used to being singled out unless it involved academics. However, the genuine warmth in Mrs. Kapoor's eyes quickly put her at ease.

"Meera," Mrs. Kapoor began, her tone thoughtful, "the change in the students this term has been remarkable. The messages, the kindness—they've brought a new energy to this place. I can't help but wonder, do you know who started it?"

Meera hesitated, her cheeks flushing. For months, she'd hidden behind the anonymity of her notes. But something in Mrs. Kapoor's knowing expression gave her the courage to speak.

"I... contributed, I guess," she admitted softly, a small, shy smile tugging at her lips. "I just wanted to help."

Mrs. Kapoor's face lit up with pride. "What you've done, Meera, is extraordinary. It takes courage to offer hope when it feels scarce, even for yourself. You've created something beautiful here. You should be proud."

The validation felt different from the kind she'd received for academic achievements—it was raw, personal, and profoundly fulfilling. As Meera walked out of the classroom, an idea she'd been toying with for weeks crystallized in her mind.

What if she created a space where kindness and mental wellness could be nurtured openly? A club where students could find solace, share their struggles, and grow together.

That evening, she sat at her desk, drafting a proposal. The club would be called The Heartfelt Initiative. She envisioned weekly group discussions, a "gratitude wall" where students could post messages, workshops on stress management, and poetry readings.

The following week, she nervously presented her idea to the principal, Mr. Chawla. His thoughtful nods as she spoke gave her confidence.

"This is a wonderful idea, Meera," he said with a smile. "Let's make it happen."

With his support, Meera reached out to her classmates. Priya was the first to join, followed by others who had been moved by the anonymous messages. At the club's first meeting, about twenty students gathered in the library.

Standing before them, Meera felt both nervous and exhilarated.

"Thank you all for being here," she began, her voice trembling slightly. "This club started with small notes, meant to remind each of us that we're not alone. Now, we have the chance to build something bigger—a community where we can truly support one another."

Ideas flowed freely. Priya suggested an anonymous advice box. Another student proposed weekly gratitude sessions. Slowly, The Heartfelt Initiative began taking shape.

Over the weeks, the club became a sanctuary. Students who had once felt invisible began sharing their thoughts. Friendships blossomed, and a collective strength emerged. One day, Ravi, a quiet student, shared his story.

"I joined this club because I needed it," he said softly. "There were days I felt invisible. But being here, knowing I'm not alone—it's made all the difference."

His words hung in the air, heavy with emotion. In response, the group offered unwavering support, creating an unspoken promise to always be there for one another.

The Heartfelt Initiative left an indelible mark on the school. Acts of kindness spread beyond the club, and even teachers noted the shift in the students' camaraderie. The bulletin board was permanently dedicated to uplifting messages, a living testament to the power of compassion.

For Meera, the journey was transformative. She no longer sought validation through perfection. Instead, she found strength in empathy and connection.

One evening, as she sat in her favorite corner of the library, Meera penned a poem for the club:

"We carry the weight, unseen and unshared,
But together we lighten what each heart bears,

For courage isn't found in being alone,
But in the voices that guide us home."

The words felt like a tribute—not just to the club, but to the resilience they had all discovered in one another.

As she looked around the library, watching her classmates laugh, read, and connect, Meera felt a deep sense of gratitude. They had all become the change they once longed for.

And in doing so, they had found something far greater than success or recognition—they had found each other.

XXII

The Next Page

Graduation day arrived faster than Meera could have anticipated. The morning was a whirlwind of caps, gowns, and last-minute hugs as she and her classmates gathered in the school auditorium. The atmosphere buzzed with a mix of excitement and bittersweet nostalgia. As Meera stood amidst her peers, she realized just how much she had transformed since first walking these hallways. The journey hadn't been easy, and there were still parts of her that felt uncertain, but today, surrounded by friends and memories, she felt ready to face whatever lay ahead.

When her name was called, she stepped onto the stage with a mixture of pride and disbelief. She had made it—not just academically but emotionally. She had endured, healed, and grown, piece by piece, note by note, friend by friend. As she glanced into the crowd, she saw her parents, Priya, and even Mrs. Kapoor smiling with unspoken pride. For the first time, Meera allowed herself to feel proud too—not of her achievements, but of the resilience and quiet strength she had cultivated over the past year.

After the ceremony, Meera and Priya wandered the school halls one last time, soaking in the memories they had made. They stopped at the bulletin board, now a collage of vibrant notes filled with hope, encouragement, and kindness—an enduring legacy of the small, anonymous act Meera had started. As she stood there, she felt a wave of emotion. Her little notes had grown into something so much bigger, something that would remain long after she was gone.

"I never thought something so small could mean so much," Meera whispered.

Priya smiled. "That's the thing about kindness—it spreads."

Before they left, Priya handed Meera a small envelope. "This is for you," she said with a grin. Curious, Meera opened it to find a beautiful journal. Its cover, embossed with gold lettering, read: For the Words Unspoken.

"It's for your poetry," Priya explained, her eyes warm. "I think the world could use a few more of your words."

Meera's throat tightened with gratitude. She hugged Priya tightly, realizing how much their friendship had carried her through. Priya had been her constant—a reminder that healing often comes through connection and understanding.

As the sun began to set, Meera walked home slowly, savoring the moment. The day had been beautiful, not just because it marked the end of an era, but because it symbolized the beginning of something new. Her journey at school had ended, but her story was far from over. Each step she took felt lighter, freer, as though she were finally ready to let the world see her as she truly was.

Once home, Meera opened the journal and ran her fingers over the words on its cover. She uncapped her pen, letting it glide across the first blank page. The words came effortlessly, spilling from a heart that had been quiet for so long but now brimmed with life and hope.

"This is only the beginning," she wrote, a quiet smile gracing her lips. "And I am ready."

XXIII

A Voice Unveiled

The weeks after graduation felt like a strange mixture of liberation and longing. Life had slowed down, and Meera found herself caught in a liminal space between her past and future, unsure of what came next. Her parents were supportive, encouraging her to take time before college to explore her passions. Despite their reassurances, an emptiness lingered—the absence of routine and the structure that school had once provided.

One quiet afternoon, Meera decided to visit her favorite spot—the small library where she had left so many anonymous notes. The library remained unchanged, a sanctuary filled with rows of worn books, silent stories, and memories. As she wandered through the aisles, she wondered how many students would stumble upon her notes, small echoes of her journey left behind to offer comfort and connection.

She took her usual seat by the window, pulling out the journal Priya had gifted her. The warm afternoon light spilled onto its pages as she flipped through her recent entries—poems, reflections, moments of doubt, and small victories. With each passing page, her words seemed more open, more fearless. What had started as an outlet had become a journey of self-discovery, documenting her pain, growth, and newfound hope.

As she sat there, lost in her thoughts, a familiar voice broke the silence. "I had a feeling I'd find you here," Mrs. Kapoor said with a kind smile, taking a seat across from Meera.

Surprised, Meera greeted her teacher, who added, "I've heard about those notes you've been leaving around the library. You've made quite an impact, you know."

Meera blushed, a bit shy. "It was just something small," she murmured. "I never thought it would mean much."

Mrs. Kapoor's expression softened. "Small acts often have the biggest impact, Meera. Sometimes, the quietest gestures are the ones that touch people the most deeply. You've created something special—a reminder that kindness exists, even in silence."

Her teacher's words resonated deeply, making Meera realize how far she had come—not just in her own healing, but in offering hope to others. Gratitude welled up in her heart, not only for Mrs. Kapoor's encouragement but for the struggles that had brought her to this point.

Taking a deep breath, Meera decided to share something she had kept private until now. "Mrs. Kapoor, I've been working on a poetry collection. It's... personal. About struggles and resilience. I don't know if it's any good, but it's something I've felt compelled to write."

Mrs. Kapoor's face lit up with encouragement. "I'd love to read it someday, Meera. Don't underestimate the power of sharing your story. Sometimes, people need exactly what you have to offer."

That night, Mrs. Kapoor's words stayed with Meera, opening up a possibility she hadn't allowed herself to consider before. For the first time, she wondered if her words had a place beyond her journal—if they could reach others who might need a reminder that they weren't alone.

The following week, she returned to the library with her notebook, ready to make a decision. Sitting at her favorite table, she read through her poems. Each one brought back memories—some painful, some healing—but together, they painted a picture of her journey. As she reached the final page, Meera realized she was ready to take the next step. Her collection wasn't just about her; it was about reaching others who were silently fighting their own battles.

She spent days refining her poems, organizing them, and writing a heartfelt preface about the anonymous notes she'd left in the library. This collection would be her tribute to anyone struggling in silence, searching for hope.

One evening, after completing the manuscript, Meera submitted it to a small publishing platform she had found online. Along with her poems, she included a message about her journey, explaining what the collection meant to her. Hitting the "submit" button felt surreal, as if she were releasing a piece of herself into the world, but it also felt profoundly right.

A few weeks later, she received a message from the platform. They wanted to publish her collection. The words on the screen didn't feel real at first, like a dream she hadn't dared to imagine. The book would be released in a simple format, but it would be out there, accessible to anyone who might need it.

The day her book arrived, Meera held it in her hands, tracing the title embossed on the cover: Unseen Battles. The weight of it felt both strange and familiar. She was no longer the girl hiding behind silence. She had found her voice and chosen to share it, turning her struggles into something meaningful.

Standing in her room, she opened the book to the final page, reading the dedication she had written:

"To those who fight in silence, know that you are never truly alone. There is strength in your battle and beauty in your resilience. Keep going."

As she closed the book, Meera felt an overwhelming sense of peace. Her journey wasn't over—in many ways, it was only just beginning. She looked out the window, watching the world unfold before her, and felt ready for whatever lay ahead.

XXIV
Echoes of Strength

With *Unseen Battles* now in the hands of others, Meera's life began to take on a new rhythm. There was a certain calmness in her days, a feeling of lightness she hadn't experienced before. People she had never met started reaching out to her online, sharing their own stories of silent struggles, battles fought in solitude, and the small victories that had kept them going. Meera was moved by the sheer vulnerability in their messages, each one a reminder that her own story was a thread in a vast tapestry of human resilience.

One evening, as she was scrolling through comments on her latest post, she saw a message from someone whose name was familiar—Mrs. Kapoor. She had read Unseen Battles and left a simple but profound comment: "You've given a voice to what so many have kept silent. Thank you, Meera, for being brave enough to share." Her heart swelled with gratitude for her teacher, who had always seen the potential in her, even when she couldn't see it in herself.

But beyond the online messages, the book started to impact her life in unexpected ways. One day, a young girl approached her while she was shopping for stationery. The girl looked about fifteen, with wide eyes and a nervous smile.

"Are you Meera?" she asked hesitantly.

Meera smiled, nodding. "Yes, that's me."

The girl held up a copy of *Unseen Battles* and said softly, "I... I wanted to thank you. I'm going through something similar, and your words... they've helped me understand that it's okay to struggle."

They shared a quiet moment, and Meera felt as if she were looking at her younger self—a girl in need of hope and reassurance. She placed a comforting hand on the girl's shoulder. "Remember," she said gently, "strength isn't in pretending we're fine. It's in finding the courage to keep going, even when it's hard."

The girl's eyes shone with gratitude, and as they parted, Meera felt as if she'd been given a glimpse of how powerful words could be. She was no longer just helping herself; she was a part of a much larger journey, offering the comfort and solidarity that she had once so desperately needed.

A few weeks later, Meera received an email from the head librarian at her school, inviting her to give a talk about *Unseen Battles*. She hesitated at first, afraid of standing in front of an audience and baring her soul. The thought of sharing her struggles, even in hindsight, made her heart race. But then, she remembered all the people her words had already touched, and she realized that this was her chance to go beyond the pages of her book. Perhaps this was her next step—to not only share her words but to be present, standing in her truth and allowing others to do the same.

The day of the talk arrived, and as she walked into the library, she felt a familiar wave of anxiety, but this time, it was tempered by a newfound strength. Rows of students, teachers, and a few familiar faces filled the room. Mrs. Kapoor sat in the front row, smiling encouragingly, her presence a reminder of the support she'd had along the way.

Taking a deep breath, Meera began, "When I was going through a difficult time, I used to think I was the only one who felt that way. But as I started to write Unseen Battles, I realized that so many of us are going through similar struggles, often in silence. This book is for everyone who has ever felt alone in their battles."

As she spoke, she shared not just the struggles that had shaped her but also the moments of courage, the small acts of kindness, and the notes that had helped her find strength. She talked about the library notes she had once hidden for others to find, each one a lifeline for someone struggling quietly. She shared how each of those messages had become a part of her healing, and how sharing her story had allowed her to connect with others in ways she had never imagined.

Looking around, she could see students nodding, a few wiping their eyes, and teachers watching with expressions of understanding. For a moment, she saw herself reflected in the faces of so many others—people who, like her, had fought silent battles and had come seeking connection and understanding.

After the talk, a line of students formed, each waiting to speak to her, some to thank her, others to share their own stories. Meera listened to each one, offering words of encouragement and support. She found that each story, each shared moment, gave her strength, deepening her resolve to keep creating, keep connecting.

That evening, Meera walked home with a heart full of gratitude. She no longer felt like the girl hiding in silence, struggling alone. She had become a beacon, her story a light in the darkness that others could follow. And as she looked up at the night sky, she thought of her journey—not just the battles she had fought, but the strength she had found, and the lives she had touched.

In that moment, she knew she was no longer just surviving. She was thriving, empowered by the knowledge that her words, her story, had made a difference. And for the first time, she felt a profound sense of peace, a quiet acceptance of herself, her journey, and the endless possibilities that lay ahead.

XXV

Ripples of Resilience

As Meera stood by her window, gazing out at the sunrise, a deep sense of peace settled within her—a calm that had eluded her for so long. Her story, once locked within her heart, had finally been shared, and through that sharing, she had not only healed herself but also helped others. The walls she had built around herself, once insurmountable, now felt like faded memories. Each new dawn brought a fresh perspective, a gentle reminder of how far she had come.

That morning, Meera walked to school with a quiet joy she hadn't felt in years. She moved through the halls with her head held high, aware of the whispers and glances but unbothered by them. She had embraced her story—every imperfect, painful, and beautiful part of it. She had faced her inner battles, fought against the relentless pressure, and had finally found a way to channel her pain into something meaningful.

During her free period, Meera made her way to the library. The librarian, who had witnessed Meera's dedication to her small, anonymous notes, greeted her with a warm smile. Over the past weeks, they had exchanged many quiet smiles, each recognizing the other as a silent ally in the world of words.

"Something tells me you've found a new strength, Meera," the librarian said gently. "You've inspired so many here, and I don't think you even realize it."

Meera nodded, feeling a rush of gratitude. "I never imagined sharing my story would mean this much, to me or anyone else. It's... freeing, you know?"

"Your courage will ripple out to those who need it," the librarian replied. "And you, my dear, will keep growing."

Just then, Mrs. Kapoor entered the library. Her familiar smile lit up her face when she saw Meera. Mrs. Kapoor had been one of the first to believe in her, and Meera knew she owed much of her journey to her teacher's unwavering encouragement. Mrs. Kapoor took Meera's hands in hers, her eyes sparkling with pride.

"Meera," she said, her voice soft but filled with emotion, "I hope you know how proud I am of you. You've faced something many adults struggle with. You've given others strength, even when you felt you had none left for yourself."

Meera's throat tightened, but she managed a nod. "Thank you, Mrs. Kapoor. Your belief in me made all the difference."

As they spoke, a small group of students approached. Each one held a piece of paper—letters, notes, or poems. Meera smiled, realizing that these were the students who had been touched by her words, by her courage to share her journey. They handed her their notes, each one expressing gratitude, empathy, or a shared understanding. The weight of these words—written by others who had walked their own difficult paths—felt like a gift.

With newfound courage, Meera stood at the front of the library and invited the students to join her. She felt their energy, their silent strength, as they gathered, and she began to read a few of the anonymous notes aloud. Each word was a reminder that struggles could connect, rather than divide, and that even in silence, they had all found a way to be heard. It was a beautiful, collective release of emotions, and the library filled with a shared warmth—a quiet celebration of resilience.

As the session ended, Meera lingered in the library, her heart full of gratitude. She realized that in telling her story, she had begun a ripple effect that would go on to inspire others. Her once-closed world had opened up, and the weight she had carried was now shared among those she had touched. While she knew she would still face challenges, she also knew that she had built the strength and resilience to handle them.

That evening, Meera returned home and opened her poetry notebook, turning to the last page where she had written a dedication to those who struggled in silence. She added a new line:

"To those who gave me the courage to keep going—thank you. Together, we find our light."

As Meera closed the notebook for the last time, a quiet determination bloomed within her. She had learned that struggles didn't define her—they shaped her. Each setback had been a stepping stone, leading her to this newfound strength. Even in the loneliest battles, hope was always within reach, as long as she looked for it.

She whispered softly, as if to herself and anyone who might be silently fighting their own battles:

"To anyone who feels lost, who feels unseen—keep going. You're stronger than you realize. There's beauty in every scar, courage in every step forward, and light waiting at the end of every dark road."

With that thought, Meera faced forward, ready to embrace whatever lay ahead. Her journey was far from over—it had only just begun.

ACKNOWLEDGEMENTS

I would like to take this opportunity to express my deepest gratitude to everyone who supported me throughout this journey.

First, I thank myself for the perseverance and dedication to this project. The process of writing "Whispers of the Unheard" was not easy, and it required an immense amount of self-reflection and determination. I am proud of the strength I found in myself, and for allowing this story to come to life.

To the silent warriors who inspire the narrative of this book – those who face their struggles without the world knowing, yet continue to carry on. Your resilience, even in solitude, is something I can never fully express in words but will forever honor.

Lastly, I would like to extend my heartfelt appreciation to the readers. Without your support, books like this would not have a voice. Thank you for embracing these stories and for finding resonance in the silence.

Author's Note

Writing Whispers of the Unheard has been an incredibly personal journey for me. The story of Meera is one that reflects not only the struggles many face in silence but also the strength that lies in sharing our stories with the world. As a writer, I have often found solace in words, whether they are written or spoken, and this novel is my attempt to offer a voice to those who have felt unheard.

Throughout Meera's journey, I wanted to capture the complexity of inner battles—those moments when we feel disconnected from ourselves and the world around us. It is my belief that healing often begins when we allow ourselves to be vulnerable, and I hope that this book offers some comfort to anyone who has ever felt alone in their struggles.

I owe a great deal of gratitude to those who have shared their own stories with me—stories of resilience, hope, and overcoming adversity. You have inspired this book in ways words cannot fully express. I hope that Whispers of the Unheard serves as a reminder that no matter how silent our battles may seem, there is always strength in finding connection, in sharing our experiences, and in embracing the journey of growth.

Thank you for allowing Meera's story to become part of your own. I hope it brings you as much peace and understanding as it has brought me.

Disha